THE
ORDER
OF THE
TREES

THE
ORDER
OF THE
TREES

KATY FARBER

GREEN WRITERS PRESS
Brattleboro, Vermont

Printed in the United States

1 0 9 8 7 6 5 4 3 2 1

Green Writers Press is a Vermont-based publisher whose
mission is to spread a message of hope and renewal through
the words and images we publish. Throughout we will adhere
to our commitment to preserving and protecting the natural
resources of the earth. To that end, a percentage of our
proceeds will be donated to the environmental activist groups.
Green Writers Press gratefully acknowledges support from
individual donors, friends, and readers to help support the
environment and our publishing initiative.

Giving Voice to Writers & Artists Who Will Make the World a Better Place
Green Writers Press | Brattleboro, Vermont
www.greenwriterspress.com

ISBN: 978-0-9909733-1-7

To my students at Rumney Memorial School:
for their courage, joy, humor, kindness, and
encouragement.

And for my sweet family. I love you more than
all the stars in the sky.

Chapter 1

CEDAR SWALLOWED HARD. The fluorescent classroom lights flooded the room, causing her to squint. She walked up the rows of desks, past the kids milling around their cubbies, gathering books. A sea of talking, giggles. Kids who felt comfortable. Kids who had friends. She made her way almost like a deer, as if walking heavily would disrupt the normal scene around her. Barely breathing, she made it to the front of the room. A little sign perched on the wooden desk said Mrs. Doneaway.

Cedar stood, rooted to the ground. Moments passed. Kids were moving around behind her, getting settled for class, bustling, moving the air like tiny tornados. She heard, "Who's that?" and "Look, it's tree girl!" in a small sea of voices. Cedar forced a small cough.

"Oh. Sorry." Mrs. Doneaway looked up from behind thick black glasses. Her eyes flickered on Cedar's wild mane of hair, her dirty T-shirt, ripped pants. "You must be Cedar. The one we've heard so much about. It is excellent you can join us." She said all of this while compiling papers on her desk.

You see, Cedar had been homeschooled before this year. But that isn't even half of it.

Cedar was different. And she was well known, but unknown, all the same.

The talk of Middlesex was that her parents found her, surrounded by a blanket of moss, under a giant white cedar tree near the Worcester Mountain trail. The story goes that the baby lay there, cooing, bubbling over with life, under a small pocket of roots. It was as though the tree itself had yielded the little child. Her soon to be parents nearly tripped over her while hiking one morning, and rubbed their eyes, making sure the baby was real. As Sara picked her up, the baby nuzzled into her, leaving sticky sap on her shirt. Kevin was outraged that someone could leave a child there, alone in the woods. They must call the police, find these irresponsible parents, and give this child over to

Child Protective services immediately. But from the moment Sara held her, covered in sap and specks of moss, she was unable to move. She would not put the baby down, or even respond to her husband's requests, and finally demands. Sara only quietly mumbled and sang to the small girl in her arms, whom she quickly named Cedar.

Once home, Kevin called their friends to try to help his wife let go of the child, but she would hear nothing of it. She rocked the baby, who seemed unhappy the moment she was brought inside their rural home. So she brought the rocker and Cedar out on the deck, and remained there well into the evening, rocking and singing to the tiny baby.

After Sara refused to go to work on Monday, Kevin started to accept his fate. That night, Sara held the baby up to the orange moonlight shining through their bedroom window. Their beauty, their oneness took his breath away. He stared, and squinted, for in that soft light, they seemed to be glowing. Shimmering. In that moment, he knew Cedar was supposed to be with them.

Kevin came to his wife, and put his arm around her waist.

"How is our sweet Cedar doing tonight?" Cedar's mom smiled brightly in recognition, hugging him sideways, and said, "Our little baby Cedar is a wonder."

❦

So was Cedar's beginning, and how she ended up with her parents, Kevin and Sara Montgomery. As she grew, Cedar remained a mystery. Her body was slender, muscular and strong, even as a child. Her eyes were wide, and she nearly never blinked, always showing those deep brown, earthy eyes; eyes that seemed like sparkly magic. And she ran. She ran deep into the woods in Middlesex at an early age. They would find her laughing, singing, walking amongst the trees as if they were long-lost friends.

The kids at Chester School knew that Cedar was different, even though they had not been in school with her until this year. Most knew the story of how she was found. Of course there were newspaper articles, TV stories, and the like. In the earlier grades, Cedar came and went for special classes in the school. Kids stared at her unblinking eyes, and made fun of the dirt underneath her fingernails and her wild brown mane of hair. The older she grew, the more time she spent in the woods behind Sara and Kevin's Middlesex home. She took books with her into the forest, and would read for hours.

By the time she entered sixth grade, and made the long walk up to Mrs. Doneaway's desk, Cedar looked almost identical to her namesake. Her skin glowed with an olive brown color, and her muscles were stretched over long limbs. Her brown hair almost reached her bottom, and flew out wildly in all directions most of the time. And her wide eyes remained her most unique and disturbing feature. Many people couldn't look at her for longer than a few seconds before blinking and looking away. With eyes of deep mahogany brown and streaks of red and orange, Cedar could see into your soul, it seemed.

Cedar's time for homeschooling had come and gone. Her parents thought she was ready to try regular school, to spend time with her peers. It was exactly like being dumped on another planet. Although she made it through that first day, and week, she still felt like an alien.

In her second week in Mrs. Doneaway's class, Cedar looked across the classroom at Phillip, another new student. He sat behind thick glasses, with his matted hair combed behind his ears. He was pale, and sat with his head between his hands.

"Hey Phillip," Cedar whispered during math, "what's wrong?"

He looked up, his face slightly greenish. Not many people actually spoke to him. He had just moved to the Chester school, and didn't have any friends. He and his parents moved around quite a bit. He glanced at Cedar nervously, as if this might be a trick, then said, "My stomach. It's been hurting all morning. I wanted to stay home, but my mom had to work."

"Listen," Cedar whispered, leaning over and avoiding Mrs. Doneaway's glance, "take one of my ginger candies. It's good for your stomach. And do you have any tea at home?"

"I don't know."

"Well, drink some tea with peppermint or chamomile in it, that should help."

"What are you, some kind of plant doctor?"

"Well, no, I just trust plants more than pills is all," Cedar said, her lips turning up slightly, her wild eyes dancing.

At that, Phillip cracked a small smile, and took some of the ginger candies from her hand.

Later at recess, Phillip found his way to Cedar's side as she walked through a field, fingering the fall blooms of black-eyed Susans and Queen Anne's lace. She barely looked up at him, as she turned from plant to plant, her hair flying around in the wind. The afternoon sun danced around her, the sky beamed bright blue.

"How are you feeling?" she said.

"Much better. Those candies were strong, but good. Did you make them?"

"Yeah," Cedar said. "Ginger has been used for thousands of years to settle stomachs, aid digestion and stop motion sickness. You just have to get the right amount, or it can give you heartburn."

"How do you know about all this stuff?"

"I read," Cedar said, "and I walk around the woods, looking, and listening."

She turned to face Phillip, her brown eyes

boring right through him. He looked down, pretending to look at the flowers. The clouds, puffy and full, watched.

"Is it true, what they say about you? That you were found in the Worcester woods?"

"I guess so," Cedar answered. "I don't remember, of course. But I do like the forest better than a lot of people."

Phillip smiled. Cedar was nothing like the other girls.

❀

Weeks went by, as a shy, new friendship was born. Phillip and Cedar would spend recess building shelters, collecting rocks or stomping in the small stream by the school. In class, they each quietly endured Mrs. Doneaway's stern voice while waiting for recess, staring outside. At night, sometimes they talked on the phone. Phillip told Cedar about his mom, her search for a new job, and his hot-headed dad. Like a sponge filling with water, life got a little bit easier for both of them.

One day, in science class, Cedar passed a note to Phillip. Other kids snickered and stared while he read it.

"Would you like to join the Order of the Trees? It's a club I started. We meet every other night at 5:00 P.M. near the Cedar tree where I was found."

Cedar looked over at Phillip, a tentative smile blooming on her lips. This was her first real friend. She failed to mention that she was the Order's only member.

He nodded silently. Phillip was never invited anywhere.

As they walked out of the classroom to the bus together, Cedar heard Miranda say loudly behind them, "Oh look, isn't that sweet, Tree Girl finally has a friend." Her smooth and well-combed pony-tail bobbed as she spoke, packed into a group of her friends.

"Too bad it's nerdy Phillip. They should have a lot in common!"

The girls laughed loudly as they walked toward the same bus.

Phillip's face turned red, and Cedar stared at them walking away.

"Just ignore them," she said.

"I see why you prefer the trees," Philip said, still red.

"So I'll see you tonight? At the Worcester trailhead?"

Chapter 2

The night was cool and damp. The trees were just starting to change colors. They were getting that crisp, dried-out green look before they change. The light filtered softly through the woods to where Cedar was seated.

She sat under the magnificent tree where she was found. Stella, the name she'd given her tree, stood at least 150 feet high, her girth too wide to fit your arms around. Cedar had visited Stella for as long as she could remember, first with her parents; then, when she was in the fourth grade, she was allowed to go alone. It was only a quarter-mile from her house, and Phillip lived only a few curves in the dirt road from them.

Small lanterns, made from tiny candles in a glass ball jars encircled the tree, glowing. Cedar sang softly while she waited. She wondered to herself if inviting him was a good idea. This place was hers. Her own oasis, her homeland. Did she really want to share it? The truth was she felt better in these woods, her woods, than anywhere else. She could breath more deeply, see clearly, and felt simply alive here. It had always been this way, for as long as she could remember.

She heard him coming long before she saw him. His feet crunched over fallen leaves. He walked like someone who doesn't spend time in the woods, heavy and unsure.

"Where is everyone else?" Phillip asked as he approached, and looked wide-eyed at the ring of lanterns around the tree.

"You, Phillip, are the only other human member. We have lots of tree members in the Order," Cedar offered, hoping he would go for it, and not run away. "That is, if you still want to be."

Smoke from the lanterns scented the air with lavender, a warm, welcoming smell, as Phillip looked down at Cedar, seated below the towering tree. The graying light surrounded her.

"Um, okay," Phillip said, glancing around, "I know nothing about trees. Being out here at night is kind of creepy." His eyes scanned the forest.

"You'll get used to it," Cedar said, gesturing for

him to sit down. "Just realize that you are safer out here in the forest than you would be in any town."

Phillip shuffled over to a spot under the tree.

"So, I hereby commence this meeting of the Order of the Trees. First, I'd like to welcome our newest member, Phillip Walker."

Phillip's mouth pushed into a crooked half smile.

"Phillip, meet Stella, the Queen," Cedar said, sweeping her arms widely. "She is by far the oldest tree in this part of the forest, and has seen a lot. She holds this forest together with her mighty strength and long-standing beauty."

"Okay," Phillip said, looking at Stella and Cedar as if he was seated on a bed of nails.

"And that over there is one of her daughters, Magdelin. She is young and reaching for light. Around her she has a few friends, and I'm not sure of their names yet. Maybe you can find and name a few of the boys."

"How do you know which ones are boys?"

"You just spend some time with them and then you get a sense."

Phillip nodded. His eyes twitched.

"It is time for us to inspect the health of the trees. What we do is visit the trees in this little grove, making sure they are healthy and happy. Use the lantern, look at every detail, in their bark, on their leaves and around their roots."

"I'm supposed to go by myself?" Phillip asked, his eyebrows pushing up from behind his glasses. The night was growing darker.

"I'll be right next to you, at a different tree." Cedar chuckled. She couldn't remember a time when she was uncomfortable in the woods. In the classroom, definitely, but not in the woods.

❀

After the tree inspection, Phillip and Cedar shared what they had found. Some woodpecker holes in Stella, a few insect trails and ruts in the bark on some medium-sized trees. A few of the smaller trees, Magdelin's size, had some bark rubbed off. They discussed which animals might have done the damage, like deer or moose.

"Now it is time for Silent Session. We sit here, completely silent, and listen to the sounds of the forest."

"For how long?"

"For as long as it takes."

Phillip shrugged his shoulders. The shadows and fading light crept around him.

Cedar lay back on a bed of moss and leaves, listening. To her, the sounds of the forest at night were a symphony more beautiful than any human-made instruments. She closed her eyes and focused completely on the forest music.

The first sounds rolled in, dull and muffled. The leaves shook slightly with the breeze, a tiny quiver. Next came the high-pitched chirping of the tree frogs. Trilling toads joined in. Some crickets droned in the distance. Sound came in waves, and Cedar felt them all, a smile forming on her lips. Time slowed as more sounds filled the nighttime forest.

In an instant, it shattered. A screeching, soul jostling, whistling sound came from high up in the trees.

"What was that?" Phillip's voice called into the symphony. His eyes shot open.

Chapter 3

It called again, this time louder, a fingers-on-a-chalkboard screech. The sound seemed to break apart the night air.

"Just listen!" Cedar whispered, "It won't hurt you!"

The moonlight filtered through the clouds, falling through the branches, and Cedar saw the movement. She pointed silently up. There, an animal was flying from a tree on silent wings, with a stout, stumpy head. It landed on one of Stella's huge arms, right above their heads, and let out a loud call. Cedar smiled, her hair full of leaves. Phillip's eyes bugged out as he stared up at the small brown puff of an owl. It eyed them in the moonlight, little rust-colored tufts pointing down, pivoting in a circle, and then flying off further into the forest.

Cedar turned her head to Phillip and, "A screech owl. That one usually visits me during Silent Session. Isn't it beautiful?"

They sat, the impression of the owl lingering in the air.

"Phillip?" Cedar looked at him, as he cupped his knees in his arms. A few moments passed while Cedar worried that bringing him here was a mistake.

Finally, Phillip's face broke into his small smile. "Amazing," he whispered, barely audible. And he was hooked.

They sat, the impression of the owl lingering in the air.

The next day in class, Cedar walked in and read the whiteboard.

Phillip + Cedar = TREE HUGGERS

There were hearts all around their names. Cedar burned red hot, and dropped her backpack and jacket. She scanned the room to find Miranda and Sam howling with laughter by the cubbies. As the rest of the kids came in off the bus, they looked at the board and either laughed or stared. Phillip sat at his desk, bright pink, pretending to read.

Cedar knew what to do. She walked right up to

the board, and began to erase it. The class gawked, whispered.

"Cedar Montgomery, just what do you think you're doing?" Mrs. Doneaway called from the doorway just as Cedar erased the last of the message.

"I was just erasing something that..."

"Did I ASK you to erase something on the board?"

"But someone wrote something..."

"You didn't answer my question. Did I ASK you to erase something on the board?"

Now the class was full, and Cedar stood in front of all of them, hot pinpricks of embarrassment reddening her face. She looked right at Miranda, her big brown eyes, shooting nails.

"No."

"That's right. So sit down."

Cedar walked speedily to her seat, staring at Miranda, who avoided her gaze.

Phillip didn't even look at Cedar for the entire morning in class. She squirmed in her seat, like a wild cat in a cage, wanting to escape. All morning, Miranda and Sam seemed to gloat that Cedar had gotten in trouble and they hadn't. Their voices were louder. Their laughs hurt her ears. Cedar just wanted to run to the forest. She peered out the classroom window, staring at the sheets of bright sunshine, blue sky.

In math class that afternoon, Cedar was working in her book when the pain started. First, she thought it was just a headache from all the attention earlier in the morning. She tried shaking her head, and focusing on equivalent fractions.

It didn't work.

At the base of her neck came a white-hot pain that caused her to drop her pencil on the floor. Rubbing her neck, she bent over to pick it up. Did I strain my neck sleeping? She wondered. She saw clouds when she sat back up. Pain burst in little bubbles in the corners of her eyes.

Some kids noticed as she shook her head, rubbed her neck.

Just then another a bright, white light seemed to shine on Cedar, causing shooting pain up her neck. It spread like a wildfire, winding though her neck, down into her shoulders and torso. She inhaled a quick breath, twisting in her seat, staring at her math book page. She had never felt pain like this before. Over and over she tried to read the same line, and she wasn't sure how long she was like that before she heard something at the end of a long, white tunnel. Muffled voices. Harsh.

"Cedar! Cedar, are you there? Earth to Cedar, come in Cedar!"

She realized the voice at the end of the tunnel was Mrs. Doneaway's.

Chapter 4

The whole class, except for Phillip, erupted in laughter and snickers. Cedar snapped back to reality and looked around. Phillip caught her eye; his face was tight with worry. She didn't remember the last few minutes at all. The only thing she remembered was bright, searing pain.

"Cedar, where have you been? You haven't done a lick of math in the past twenty minutes," Mrs. Doneaway said. She towered over Cedar, her body looming in crisp clothes.

Cedar felt the blood draining to her toes. Her head felt heavy, like it might roll around without her knowing. A dull thumping pain throbbed at the base of her neck.

"I . . . I don't feel so good." Cedar said.

"Well, you could've said something sooner, Cedar. Go to the nurse." Mrs. Doneaway turned her back and walked up to the board.

So much for sympathy. Phillip watched as

Cedar made her way slowly out of the classroom, the normal fire in her eyes dimmed.

❧

The phone rang in the Montgomery's little cabin in the Worcester woods.

"Cedar?" Phillip asked.

"Hi Phillip," Cedar said, walking to her room.

"Are you okay?"

"Yeah. I'm fine. I just came home and slept. But I never do that. I really have no idea what happened." Cedar sat on her bed, stroking DaVinnci, her cat, lazily.

"You looked so pale, and so … different."

"Phillip, how long was Mrs. Doneaway saying my name?"

"For a while. She probably said it seven or eight times."

"Wow, Phillip," Cedar said, leaning back on her pillows.

"What?"

"I only heard the last one."

"What do you mean? Were you just spacing out?"

"No," Cedar said, her hand stopping in the middle of DaVinnci's back, "no, I was just not there."

"You must just be sick. You should make up some of your herbal mumbo-jumbo to fix you and go to bed."

"What about the Order meeting?"

"What about it? You shouldn't go out in the woods tonight. It's cold out there."

"I'll be fine."

"I really don't think you should," Phillip said. He waited.

"That was rough today. Those girls."

Phillip hesitated. The line was quiet.

"I'll see you there at 5:00," Cedar said, and hung up.

Under a blanket of slate grey sky, the forest was dark. Cedar sat, leaning against Stella, thinking. What happened to me today? She thought. She remembered the bright white light, the climbing, searing pain, and shuddered. She curled up closer to Stella's deep, dark bark, waiting. In the cradle of

Stella, her body relaxed. Cool night air filled her lungs, and she was grateful for it.

"Hi," Phillip said, approaching in the twilight, "You okay? You look out of it."

Cedar pulled out of her thoughts. "Oh yeah, I'm fine."

"I told you, you shouldn't be out here tonight," he said, settling in on the ground beside her.

"I'm fine, Phillip, stop worrying!"

He smiled his small smile, pushed his hair from his eyes.

"I'd like to call this meeting to order," Cedar said. They settled in for the second meeting of the Order of the Trees.

After silent session, and a visit from the screech owl, Phillip and Cedar leaned against Stella.

"Were you born here, I mean, actually born? What do your parents say?" Phillip said.

"They tell me I am part of the forest. They say I was magic. That I was given to them by the tree. They get a starry, far-away look when they talk about it."

"Do you think that?" Phillip asked quietly. He didn't want to upset her.

"Well, I do love these trees. My trees. Especially Stella."

They were quiet. "I like them too," he paused, "but what do you think really happened? You know, I've taken health class…"

"You can just stop right there. I have no idea. I have two great parents and some enchanted woods. It just matters that I'm here, right?"

"Right," Phillip said. He smiled into the night. This girl, he thought, is of the trees.

Later, during the inspection of the trees, Phillip called to Cedar.

"What do you make of this?" Phillip gestured to bright orange tape wound around a small maple tree.

Cedar's face fell. "Someone else has been here recently," she said. "Did you see this the other day, during the last inspection?"

"No, and I did walk over here because I remember that large boulder. I would've noticed."

Cedar fingered the ribbon. "It looks new. There's no wear on it, no dirt."

"Why would someone be marking the trees? Our trees?" Phillip asked, his eyebrows pushing upwards.

A cloud pushed over the last of the twilight, sending them into sea of deep grey forest.

Chapter 5

Cedar woke up suddenly, breathing hard, soaked with sweat. She searched her mind, but couldn't remember her dream. Whatever it had been about, it disturbed her. She got ready for school quickly, and filed out to the kitchen.

"Morning, Cedar. Want some toast?" Cedar's mom kissed her on the forehead, hugging her sideways. "Whoa, honey, you are clammy. Are you sick again? Is everything all right?"

Cedar nodded, and said, "Just a bad dream."

"Why don't you have a little tea before you catch the bus? Something to settle your nerves?"

"No time Mom, thanks. See you tonight." Cedar pushed through the wooden door, past the fading gardens, and up Bear Swamp road to her bus stop.

At school, Cedar slipped in silently, as she'd learned to do, trying to go unnoticed. Unnoticed, that is, to everyone except for Phillip.

He gave her a small wave, but didn't look for too long. Last time, they'd been caught, made fun of. Cedar wondered if she embarrassed him. If he was truly her friend, he wouldn't be embarrassed. She wondered if they really were friends. She hoped so.

Math time came and went, the usual students being their usual selves. Cedar remained uneasy, anxious. Her stomach pulsed with a dull, nervous ache.

At snack time, Cedar went back to the reading area, hoping Phillip would join her. At least they could have a little privacy there. He came back, looking around quickly as he walked.

"Hey," he whispered, "how are you? Feeling OK?"

"Yeah," Cedar lied, eating ginger candies, "How about you?"

"I'm fine, I just don't want any more trouble from Mrs. Doneaway or those girls." He looked around from behind his glasses until his eyes settled on the two girls by the cubbies.

He is embarrassed, Cedar thought. They were silent for a few moments. Phillip looked at his feet. The air seemed stuck, unsure, between them.

"Ah, don't worry about them. They aren't even

members of the Order," Cedar looked down. Her head pulsed, blood pounding.

"So what do you think the orange tape was all about?" Phillip asked.

"The Order? What, are you guys in some sort of cult? Do you have your own language?" Miranda and Sam had crossed the room and appeared right behind them, eavesdropping. Sam let out her barking laugh.

Cedar looked up, eyes steady. "None of your business."

Miranda looked at Cedar, measuring the challenge. "Right," she said. "This is Tree Girl, the one found abandoned in the woods. Of course, so much of your mysterious life is none of my business. I guess it's none of my business that you're in a cult, but don't take Phillip down with you." She looked at Phillip, and batted her eyes. "He doesn't need to be part of your freak show."

"Go away," Cedar said, her gaze solid as a tree.

Miranda's eyes flickered to Cedar, and she turned towards Phillip, squaring her shoulders. Her hair was pinned up delicately with clips and sprayed into place. Lip gloss glistened on her lips as she spoke. "Phillip. I'm having a party Friday night. If you've had enough of cult girl here, and you are ready for some normal friends, please join us."

Phillip froze, shifting his glance between them all. The whole class was listening; the air in the room seemed to stop moving.

"And Cedar? You might want to pay more attention to getting dressed tomorrow." Miranda pointed to Cedar's feet. One of her socks was a bright blue, the other, red. Sam's loud laughter continued as they paraded across the classroom, proud of their conquest.

Cedar burned inside, a forest fire.

At lunch, Cedar sat down at a table alone. Phillip was still in line. Minutes seemed to take forever as she watched him make his way through it. He started walking towards her table, and Cedar felt a little light come into her heart. Maybe she really did have her first friend.

"Hey," he said, sitting down. "I'm really sorry about what happened."

"It wasn't your fault."

"I know, but I just feel bad that they…"

"Invited you to their party? Go ahead, Phillip, if you want to."

This threw him. He was speechless. "Are you sure you wouldn't mind?"

"I just have to tell you, I think they are using you. Using you to make fun of me."

"Oh, I see, I'm not cool enough for an invitation, am I?" Phillip's eyes narrowed, his face getting red.

"No," Cedar said evenly, "I think you are. I do. I just don't want you to get hurt."

And like a door opening suddenly, there it was again. The white light shot upwards through her, careening from her toes to her skull. Cedar grabbed her head, squinted, as what felt like shards of glass pierced her body, again and again.

"Cedar? Cedar?" Phillip called. He was at the end of a long tunnel of sound.

She stood up, walked like a drunk across the room, barely in control of her body. She stumbled a bit, wavering, and ran right into Savannah Westerberg, whose tray went flying, spaghetti sailing across the cafeteria, splattering the floor red.

They both fell like rag dolls, and Savannah

landed directly in the spaghetti sauce. The cafeteria erupted in laughter, and gasps. It looked like a scene from a horror movie. Savannah bounced back up, brushing herself off, shot a look at Cedar, and scrambled for the door. Cedar sat up, her head between her hands, not moving. She started waking up from her pain, pulling herself out.

A teacher went to her, and helped her up. She shook her head, rubbed her temples.

"I'm fine," Cedar said.

"We'll just take you to the nurse to be sure," the teacher said, his arm around her shoulders. The whole room watched as she was led out of the cafeteria. Cedar looked back as the teacher opened the heavy metal door, but she didn't see Phillip.

Chapter 6

"Is Cedar there?"

"Hi Phillip," Mrs. Montgomery answered, and dishes clanked in the background. "She's here, but she's up in bed. I think she's sleeping. I don't know what's gotten…"

"Could you check?"

"Well, Phillip, I think she needs her rest."

"It's just that I wanted to tell her something."

"She knows, you won't meet in the woods tonight, not after today."

Phillip was silent on the line. He didn't know she knew about the Order.

"Thanks for your call, Phillip." Click.

The next morning, right off the dirt road and a bit into their tunnel of trees, three men set to work building a small platform to park the yellow, angular machines. Both the men and the machines were getting ready for the big job of clearing the forest.

Unnatural sounds echoed through the Worcester Woods that morning. Birds took flight, frantic, and even the wind seemed to hurry by. The truck doors clanked open and shut. The engines ran, the saw hummed, the reverse single beeped. Men joked, cursed and moved trees and earth.

All of it in only a hour or two. That was all that was needed to cut down seven trees at the beginning of the trail, and to move the earth from its home under the downed leaves and dew into a neat, flat rectangle. The trees were cut up, heaved into a truck, taken away. Three bulldozers and other equipment were lined up neatly on the new parking area, ready for the next step.

The sun glinted off their yellow, hard metal. All was quiet again in the Worcester Woods after they left. But they would never again be the same. The process had begun.

❀

Cedar walked into school the next day looking ragged. Her hair was matted and in knots, and she walked slower than normal. Phillip watched her come in, and his eyes followed her to her seat. She didn't even look up, look for him.

Finally, in math, Cedar turned around, and looked at him. Her wild eyes were dull and muted, red. He mouthed, "Are you okay?" to her, and she nodded slowly, and turned back around.

Later in the morning, language arts class began. Cedar knew she had to present her newspaper article to the class, summarizing the important parts. She read the article again to herself. I can do this, she thought. Just focus. You're fine.

Phillip picked up today's paper. His summary wasn't due until tomorrow. He scanned the front page, then turned to the Local section. He read the headline twice, and drew in a quick breath. He looked up at Cedar, whose eyes were downcast, reading fervently, and reviewing her notes. "No, no, no," he said, as he started reading the article.

"Okay class, it's time for summary presentations. Please put away your choice reading, and give your attention to our presenters."

Phillip didn't budge. His eyes were locked to the page.

"Do I have a volunteer to go first?"

"Cedar!" Phillip called in a strained whisper, "Cedar!" He was going to pass her the newspaper— or hold it up so she could see what it said.

"That was nice of you to volunteer your friend, Phillip." Mrs. Doneaway smirked as she walked up the aisle. "Cedar, please start us off."

Cedar slowly made her way to the front of the classroom. Her hair was matted to her head, and her face was a shade of pale ivory. Her eyes were lined with red and her cheeks seemed pulled in, hollow. Her T-shirt was wrinkled and worn. Miranda and Sam snickered as she stood there, looking down at her papers.

"Anytime, Cedar, anytime," Mrs. Doneaway's voice called, soaked in sarcasm.

Phillip watched, the newspaper clutched tightly in his hand.

"Increased mercury levels in fish can harm our health," she read, her voice monotone. "A new study says that the increased level of mercury in tuna and salmon can…"

Cedar stared down at the paper, and started swaying slightly. Phillip held his breath as her voice got softer and softer. Miranda shot Sam a look of excitement.

Cedar started rocking back and forth, her voice barely audible. Her eyes were slits, and she read in a quiet murmur.

Phillip held his breath. Hang in there, Cedar. Just finish this and I'll show you the paper.

"Cedar, we can't hear you any—"

Mrs. Doneaway stood up suddenly as Cedar's head rolled forward first, then the rest of her body followed, as if in slow motion. She came down hard, face first on the linoleum floor with a sickening smack. In an instant, Mrs. Doneaway was by her side, holding her head up. Cedar's eyes were closed.

Phillip was standing, staring.

"Somebody get the nurse! Quick!" Mrs. Doneaway yelled in a high-pitched, piercing call. Her eyes were wide, scanning the class for help.

Phillip threw down the paper and ran to the office. It landed on the floor, its headline unnoticed. It read, "New development planned for the Worcester Woods."

Chapter 7

Phillip sat in class, pretending to pay attention. Mrs. Doneaway talked on about ancient Egypt, and he fidgeted in his seat, wondering how Cedar was doing. He stared at the clock, willing it forward. He had seen the ambulance come and take Cedar away on a stretcher. Her face looked a shade of bone grey, and her eyes remained closed as they wheeled her out. The class seemed like a fog had settled around them. They were quiet, subdued. Mrs. Doneaway even seemed out of sorts. She lacked her spirited sarcasm and quiet disdain. Her eyes flickered to Cedar's empty seat, and the line between her eyes deepened.

Phillip couldn't stop thinking about the newspaper article. Where was this new development planned? Why hadn't they heard about it? What would happen to the Order?

Phillip rubbed his eyes, and heard the bell ring. He jumped up and ran for the door. Shoving his books in his backpack in one move and throwing it over his shoulder, Phillip barely noticed Miranda in the doorway.

"Have you thought anymore about the party on Saturday?" she said, batting her eyelashes.

Phillip pushed by her; he yelled behind his back, "I've got to go!"

"Where are you going!?"

But Phillip was already out of the door, his feet pounding the hallway floor. He burst outside and stood for a moment, thinking. Just like flipping a light switch, he made his decision and ran up Shady Rill Road toward Bear Swamp.

The evening sun felt soft and warm on his back, but he paid it no notice. He ran focusing on what he was going to find. His feet thump-thumped on the dirt road, his breath rhythmic, pushing in and out.

It can't be, he thought. It's just not possible.

His glasses slid down his nose, causing him to lose his vision for a few moments. He sucked in and out, gasping for breath, trying to keep moving. As he turned up Bear Swamp, Phillip prayed he wouldn't see his mom or Cedar's parents on the road. He didn't want to answer any questions about why he was running, or why he was splattered with mud.

Please let her be okay, he thought, please. My only friend.

When he reached the Worcester trailhead, he stopped and turned in. He nearly ran right into the machines that stood like soldiers waiting. It was exactly like a punch in the gut. He rubbed his face in disbelief, trying to make sense of the platform, the missing trees, the equipment. He turned quickly away. He had to know if their forest was okay.

The trees made a colorful tunnel for him as he started walking at a brisk pace. The woods glowed, bathed in late orange light as he pushed on. The trees stared at him, silently watching.

Finally, he came around a bend and stopped dead in his tracks. He stared at their clearing, at Stella, Magdalene, Rose and the rest of the trees in their sacred place. His jaw dropped as his eyes darted between trees. Phillip held his breath, noticing the small orange ribbons tied to each tree. Some around the center, some around a small branch. He counted the trees with this marking, sweat dripping down his forehead. In the center of them all stood the wide and graceful Stella, with the same thick orange tape tied around her wide girth. The color was blindingly unnatural against her earthy brown form.

Forty-two trees in all! This has to be it, he thought, this is where the houses are going. When did all these ribbons go up? He pushed his knuckles down, heard the loud pops. Phillip looked back, and realized the trail he walked in on would be a road. Not a tunnel of beautiful trees, but a road for this new development. Pavement to their secret place. Pavement to the place where he met his first friend. He clenched his fists, took a deep breath and yelled.

"Nooooo!!!" Hot tears pushed to his eyes, and pattered down his face. The only friend he had, the only place they were safe from the world, gone.

He had to get to her. He had to tell her. But what would it do? She was sick and in the hospital, she couldn't do anything about it. Phillip rubbed his temples. The air pushed in around him.

Why was she sick? He thought. What was happening?

He looked out at the grove of trees. At Stella,

the grooves in her bark like intricate highways lead-
ing up her wide, powerful trunk. The air stopped
around him, waiting. The trees seemed to whisper
in his ear and suddenly, it was clear.

If Cedar was born under this tree, if the tree
falls, she'll die. Phillip shook his head. How could
that be true? Everything he had ever learned
screamed inside his mind that he was crazy; there
was no magic, no relationship between the impend-
ing development and Cedar's sickness. A tiny voice,
coming straight from his heart, told him it was true,
that Cedar's life was in danger and they didn't have
much time. Phillip felt the blood leave his face and
he turned into the pumpkin-colored woods to run
straight to his house.

Once he reached his parents' small rented farm-
house, he stopped to walk, to gather himself. His
T-shirt was soaked and clinging to his back. Phillip
wiped his brow with the back of his hand.

He pushed in the door, and burst into the
kitchen where his parents were getting ready for
dinner. Phillip couldn't keep in it. All in one sen-
tence he blurted out, "Cedar's in the hospital I need
to go see her right away."

So much for acting normal.

Silverware clanked on plates. "Oh!" his mom said, jumping up from setting the table, "Oh, God, Phillip, what is it now? That poor girl's been so sick."

Phillip gulped, and pushed out words. "Mom, can you give me a ride to the hospital? I just need to see if she's okay."

Phillip's mom shot her husband a look. She turned her eyes back to Phillip and raised one eyebrow. Phillip felt his face go prickly hot, turning the color of the orange sunset.

"Tomorrow's Saturday, I can catch up on sleep this weekend. I just want to be there." The heat flamed his face, deep red by now, but Phillip held his mom's gaze.

Painfully long seconds passed until Philip's mom said, "All right, all right. I can see you really care about her."

Phillip ran to his room, grabbed his backpack, shoving in random items they might need: his laptop, flashlight, blankets, the newspaper. His plan solidified in his head as he whirled around the room.

Riding to the hospital, Phillip pretended to listen as his mom talked. What if they couldn't do it?

What if they were caught? His heart pounded in his chest. Cedar was in pain, he knew, and it might not stop. It would only get worse. They couldn't help her at the hospital. They didn't know the secret, and wouldn't believe it if they did.

Trying to sound casual, Phillip said, "Mom, have you heard about the development going into the Worcester woods by the trailhead?

Glad to have something else to talk about she said, "Oh yes, its been all over the news, isn't it terrible?"

Phillip nodded, trying to keep his voice even. "What do you know about it?" He stared out the window, avoiding her eyes.

"Oh, its some businessman from Burlington, he will be developing that whole hillside, putting in a neighborhood of about 20 houses. It's such a shame. Traffic will increase on our road, but you know, it will be good for the school. More of a tax base, they say, more funding for our tiny, old school, which Lord knows we need."

"Do you know when they will start cutting the forest?" He tried to control a wince as he spoke.

His mom turned to look at him for a second—a

look that said, "Just why are you so curious?" But she continued, "Our neighbor says they'll start soon, to try to get the site ready before the snow falls. He even thinks it will be this week, because they've told him to expect logging trucks to be active on the edge of his land."

"That soon?" Phillip's heart shot up into his throat. Cedar!

"What is it, Phillip? You can play somewhere else, you know?"

"It's. Not. Playing," Phillip said. They pulled up to the hospital roundabout.

"Thanks Mom," Phillip called as he burst out the door, before she could reach over and kiss him.

"Call when you need a ride home," she called after him. The door had already slammed shut.

Phillip strode down the hospital sidewalk, thinking about how he could talk to Cedar alone, what they would do, and how she would react. Would she think he was crazy? Or would she know he was right? He walked faster.

At the hospital reception desk a woman with orange lipstick and sprayed perfect hair said, "May I help you?"

"Yes. I'd like to see Cedar Montgomery please."
His voice was shaky.

"Are you family?"

"Well, no, just, um, a friend."

"I see." She shuffled some papers, looked down.
"Visiting hours are over at 7:00 P.M. Please sign out
a few minutes before that. She's in room 316. Take
the elevator up, and turn right. It'll be the fourth
room on the left." She paused and looked at her
clock. "You'd better hurry."

Phillip looked at his watch. 6:45 P.M. He tore
down the hall, his feet clapping against the tile floor.
He pushed the elevator button three times.

"Come on!" Phillip wiped the sweat from his
brow with the back of his hand. He tapped his
foot. What if she was asleep? Busy with family? He
gulped, straightened his hair in the reflection of the
gold metal elevator door.

Bing! The door opened and Phillip sailed
through the hall, past people in wheelchairs, and
busy nurses and doctors walking as fast as he was.
He got to 316 and the door was partially closed. He
peered inside, tightening his stomach around the
butterflies. Inside Cedar lay stretched out on the

hospital bed, with an IV stuck in her arm, dripping mysterious fluid. She was looking at her parents, who had their seats pulled up around her bed. He stood there for a moment and she turned her head, as if she knew he was there. She waved him in.

"Phillip!" Sara said, jumping up, "Well, I didn't expect you. How nice of you to come!" She looked between them quickly. Kevin offered his hand for Phillip to shake.

"How is she?" he asked.

"She is doing quite fine, and can speak for herself," Cedar said, a smirk blooming across her face.

Phillip smiled for the first time in hours, and Sara offered him a seat. Cedar stared at Phillip for a moment, and his smile quickly retreated as he noticed how pale she was. You could almost see her blue blood vessels under the skin. Her eyes were red and deeply shaded underneath. She looked as though she'd been awake for days. Despite this she said, "Phillip, I'm not dead yet, so don't look at me like I am!"

He nodded and looked away quickly, unsure what to do with himself. Sara picked up on this and said, "Kevin, why don't we go down to the cafeteria and get some coffee. Kids, do you want anything? Ice cream?"

Cedar stared at Phillip while she said, "No Mom, we're fine." Phillip nodded in agreement and Kevin and Sara disappeared out the door.

"How are you really?"

"I'm OK, it's just that I don't feel like myself, and these people keep giving me medications that have nasty chemicals in them and they overpower me. I feel like an alien in my own body."

"What do they think it is?"

"They have no idea. They are going to do a bunch of scary tests on me tomorrow. Needles, X-rays, CAT scans, the works, just awful. I don't want to be here."

Phillip looked out the window onto the dark parking lot. He knew he just had to come right out and say it.

"What is it, Phillip? Did Miranda and Sam do something today?" Her face crinkled up with concern.

"No, no. It's just that I think I know why you are sick. And I don't think it has anything to do with all this." He gestured to all the medical equipment around them.

Cedar's eyes opened wider. The light seemed to shine out of them again.

"Look at this."

He handed her the crinkled-up local paper, folded open to the development article. "I went to our spot today, Cedar. There is orange tape everywhere, on Magdelin, Rose, and even … Stella. Forty-two trees. Scheduled to be knocked down any day now for that new development. I mean, you were born there, right? That is your place, your family. Maybe in some weird way, your life depends on that forest."

Cedar's eyes filled with water, and her hand reached for Phillip's. "Of course," she said quietly, "of course." She looked up at Phillip. "If Stella dies…"

Phillip strained to keep looking at her deer-like eyes. "Don't say it. We'll figure out a way to stop it."

"But how?"

Now it was Phillip's turn to be strong. "We don't have much time, but I have an idea. It is going to be incredibly risky and it may not work, but what other choice to we have?"

Cedar nodded. "Go on."

Chapter 8

When Phillip finished explaining, he looked down at his watch and said, "I have to go, Cedar. Visiting hours are over and your parents will be back any second."

Cedar nodded, her big eyes begging him not to leave her there.

"You only have one day left here if all goes as planned. You can make it. Just think about our trees, the forest. Think about Stella. And ways to make our plan work."

"I think you've already done most of that."

Sara and Kevin looked in the tiny window on the closed door and smiled.

"Ten o'clock Monday night," Phillip said, standing up.

"Ten o'clock." Tears sprouted in her eyes again.

Back at home, Phillip stared at his desk. His cat Rufus rubbed his legs, and jumped on his lap. "How will I convince these sixth graders to help us? They don't even like us," he asked Rufus as he purred and nuzzled his hand. He stared at the blank piece of paper in front of him.

He wrote, "Important Meeting at Recess. Cedar Montgomery needs our help." then crossed it out. I need to get their attention, Phillip thought. "Your classmate, Cedar Montgomery is in danger. She needs your help. Meet by the swing set at 12:30 Monday."

Phillip's hand ached as he copied the message over and over on to small slips of paper. Before he knew it, his little brother had popped up behind him.

"Whatcha doin'?" He said. His pudgy hand reached for the notes.

"Nothing Colin, get outta here."

He ushered his little brother out of the room and closed the door. "Mom," Phillip heard, "Phillip is writing notes!"

"Argh!" Phillip moaned as he slammed his fist on the table.

Before school the next day Phillip couldn't eat breakfast. His stomach squirmed as he thought of the meeting, what he'd say, and whether they'd all laugh at him. Just think about Cedar, he thought. She's suffering and will only get worse unless you do this. He readied himself for battle.

When Phillip got to school, he slid into his chair and tried to concentrate on breathing. He looked around. Mrs. Doneaway wasn't in the room yet. This was one of his chances.

He looked over to Dan Bloom, seated in the row next to him. Dan was doodling on his folder.

"Psst, Dan!" Phillip said in a forced whisper. He handed him the note across the row, his hand shaking. Dan read it and his eyes grew large. He nodded and shoved the paper deep in his pocket.

Phillip handed out five more papers before Mrs. Doneaway came charging in the room. Miranda glared at Phillip from the back corner. She whispered something to Sam who snickered.

"Is there something wrong, girls? Or are you ready to start class?"

"Oh, we're ready to start class, Mrs. Doneaway, we just wanted you to know that someone is passing notes in this class." Miranda looked at Phillip sideways, her pink glossy lips upturned slightly.

Phillip stared straight ahead, but several heads turned towards him. He face felt like it had burst into flames. Mrs. Doneaway walked slowly, her heels clicking on the way, to Phillip's desk. She paused, looked down from beneath her pointy glasses and said, "Really." She stopped for dramatic effect, and the air seemed to evaporate right out of the room. "Is that true, Phillip? Passing notes?" Each word was said as if it took up her whole mouth, and tasted good.

Phillip squirmed. "I, ah, well… " Heat rose from his forehead, beaming red.

"That's no answer, Phillip. I'm waiting." She stood right beside him and tapped her pencil on her hand.

Phillip looked around frantically. The whole class stared back, and Miranda and Sam smiled with satisfaction at the torture Phillip endured.

"No." It came out like a squeak, the smallest little sound.

"What?" She said, eyebrows raised.

"No, Mrs. Doneaway, I wasn't passing notes." Phillip said a little louder, sitting up.

"OK then. But I'll be watching just to be sure." She smiled back at Miranda, who beamed.

And she walked back towards the front of the classroom, click, click, click.

"Now class, where were we with adding fractions?"

❀

Later in the lunchroom almost everyone in the sixth grade seemed to know about the meeting. Phillip had passed out more notes at snack time, in the hallway and the bathroom. Since Cedar was out of school, Phillip had sat at his usual table for lunch, alone. But today, many kids came and sat next to him, asking questions about the meeting and commenting on the close call with Mrs. Doneaway in class. Many of them looked at him like it was the first time they were actually seeing him. He quietly repeated several times that Cedar was sick, in grave danger, and that she needed everyone's help to get better. Kids looked at him like he was a little crazy, and brave to do something like this.

Miranda plunked down next to Phillip at the cafeteria table. "How sweet. Phillip is trying to save poor little Tree Girl. Isn't that just special? What will we do, dance around a tree singing chants to save her?" Sam snorted next to her.

Phillip turned back to his grilled cheese. I'm not going to punch Miranda in the face, he told himself, I'm not.

"Aww, too afraid to speak up? Just like today with the notes? I thought you'd melt right out of your chair the way Mrs. Doneaway was looking at you. 'No,' you squeaked in that high, little voice of yours."

"Shut up," Phillip said with forced calm, staring at his tater tots.

"What you'll do for love."

"I said shut up, Miranda. Go sit somewhere else."

A few of the kids who came to sit with Phillip stared at her.

"Fine. But you won't catch me at your stupid meeting. And maybe I'll just let Mrs. Doneaway know what you're up to. Maybe she could help poor little Cedar too, huh?"

She got up, her carefully placed blond curls bouncing, and walked back to a full table. Phillip didn't watch her go.

"Don't worry about her, man," Dan Bloom said, "She's evil."

❀

Phillip splashed water on his face in the bathroom. He couldn't seem to cool himself down. Today had already been tortuously long, and Phillip hadn't even had the meeting yet. Just breathe, he thought, it'll be over soon. Cedar needs your help. Even if you end up in Mr. Busch's office. Phillip had never been in trouble at school before. He followed directions and did his homework. All this attention had caused his stomach to turn in knots. He stood over the sink, still sweating.

He looked at his watch. It was time. Kids would be filing out of classes to recess at any minute. He pulled out his note cards and looked at them one last time. Phillip took a deep breath, shoved them in his back pocket and headed outside.

Some kids were already gathered behind the play structure, standing nervously. Phillip knew he didn't have much time before the teacher would notice, become curious and make his way over to find out what was happening. He strode quickly out and several kids started following him. Phillip didn't look to see if any teachers saw him.

Now most of the sixth grade class stood behind the structure, slightly hidden from view. The fourth and fifth graders ran wildly around, barely noticing the big group. Phillip gestured for them to sit down, and crouched himself.

Phillip felt his heart hammer in his chest. He looked up at the group, and noticed Miranda and Sam leaning against a tree behind the swings. He took a deep breath, and began.

Chapter 9

As you all know, Cedar Montgomery is really sick. She is in the hospital, and she is not improving. In fact right now they are probably poking needles in her and doing all sorts of uncomfortable tests." Some kids winced and nodded, others just stared. Many of them had never heard Phillip speak, much less speak to a large group.

"And I know all of you have heard in some way where Cedar was found, out in the Worcester woods. No one ever came forward as Cedar's parents. She was found at the base of a big and beautiful tree. And what I'm about to say sounds crazy, I know. Many of you probably won't believe me. Even if you doubt what I say is true, even if you think I'm nuts, if you care about your fellow classmate Cedar, you'll ignore that logical part of your mind and join me."

Dan Brown tapped Phillip. "Mr. Phelps is coming over across the field."

"Okay. The woods where Cedar was found are about to be cut down. Including the ancient tree she was found under. Several houses are to be built there. Cedar started getting sick when all this started. She's gotten sicker as the date nears. Construction will happen within the next week."

"Yeah," Dan said, "I live right next door, and they brought in the bulldozers yesterday."

"Just what are you saying?" A girl from another class blurted out.

Phillip gulped. "I think that Cedar may die if we don't stop this. She needs your help." Phillip glanced up and saw Mr. Phelps rapidly approaching. "Be there, tomorrow, at 7:00 A.M., with your parents and everyone you can think of. Bring signs, bells, whistles. Tell everyone you know about it."

Some kids giggled, and Miranda rolled her eyes.

"And do what?" the same girl called out.

"Protest. Stop the development. Whatever it takes."

"Whatever what takes, Phillip?" Mr. Phelps asked as he approached. The group scuttled away quickly, leaving Phillip alone. Only Dan stayed behind.

"Oh, it's about a club he wants to start," Dan chimed in. "Right Phillip? An environmental club? He just had his first meeting. Lots of interest, huh?"

Mr. Phelps smiled at the boys. "That's great! You know, small groups of people can change the world!"

They nodded and Mr. Phelps walked toward the soccer field.

"Thanks," Phillip said, "that was close." Dan nodded. They were silent for a moment or two. Phillip's hands were pushed deep in his pockets.

"Dan?"

"Yeah?"

"Do you think they'll come?"

"I have no idea, man. But I'll be there." He brushed the straggly hair from his eyes as the bell rang for class. They ran down to the doors and lined up to go in. Cool wind blew the clouds across the sky, shifting. Before Phillip knew it he could feel Miranda's eyes on his face.

"So noble of you, Phillip. To stage a protest to save your dying girlfriend." She sighed dramatically. "What next, are you going to ride there on your white horse? Pick Tree Girl up by the waist and ride off into the sunset?"

Phillip ignored her, stared straight ahead.

As he tried to pass through the door, Miranda put her hand up to stop him.

"What if I tell on you Phillip? What will you do then?"

He turned to her slowly, as the line of kids built up behind them and said, "I'll do it anyway." He pushed her arm back and passed through the door.

"Ladies and gentlemen," Miranda called, "Phillip the hero!" she said sarcastically. "I don't think he can save his way out of a paper bag!"

Phillip stared at the clock in anguish. This was the longest school day of his life. His stomach rolled over again and again, threatening to charge out of his mouth right then and there. Sweat beaded on his forehead, although it was quite cool in the classroom. Mrs. Doneaway droned on about Ancient Greece, writing all over the board and expecting everyone to take detailed notes and follow her disjointed thinking. Instead, Phillip worked on his intricate plan for Cedar's escape from the hospital. From memory he drew the hospital floor she was on, labeling the rooms in between, the exits, and everything else he could remember.

He pictured Cedar on the hospital bed, propped up on her side. Her face would be twisted up in pain as they stuck a long needle deep into her spine. He could see her beautiful hair all stringy and matted, her bright deer eyes dulled in pain. Phillip remembered the day she read the summary to the class and then fell to the floor. He winced and a shiver shot up and down his spine. His notebook jumped off his desk and landed with a resounding *thwack!* on the floor. Mrs. Doneaway jumped in the air while writing on the board when she heard the unexpected sound. She did not like surprises. Kids in the class giggled, thinking he did it on purpose.

Phillip bent down quickly to grab his notebook, as Mrs. Doneaway's narrow eyes settled squarely on him.

"Phillip! It's so nice that you volunteered your notes as a model for the class!"

She walked over slowly, gathering all the tension in the room.

"Let's have a look, shall we?" Her eyes gleamed behind pointy glasses. She put out her hand for the notebook. Phillip looked pained as he handed it to her and shrugged his shoulders.

Mrs. Doneway stared at the notebook page while the class held their breath. Her eyes grew into slits, and she slammed the notebook down on his desk.

"Out of the classroom!" she bellowed, "Down to Mr. Bausch's office! And show him what you have been doing in my Social Studies class!"

Chapter 10

The color drained from Phillip's face. He gathered his notebook and stood up as if in slow motion. Dan looked at him sympathetically, but Miranda and Sam beamed. Once in the hallway, Phillip tried to slow his breathing. Just get through today, he thought. All that matters is tonight, helping Cedar. Calm down. Breathe in. Breathe out. Phillip had never been to see the principal. He didn't even think Mr. Busch knew who he was. What would his mom say?

His footsteps echoed on the tile floor. He slipped in to the office and sat down by the principal's door so quietly that the administrative assistant didn't even know he was there. After a few phone calls she finally noticed him.

"Oh! Hello there. What can I do for you?"

"I was sent here by Mrs. Doneway."

She looked at him for a moment. "Are you sure?"

Phillip nodded. She tilted her head and said,

"All right." Picking up the phone she dialed Mr. Busch. "Yes, sir, Phillip Rogers here to see you. Yes, yes. Grade 6. Yep. Mrs. Doneaway. OK?"

The door opened suddenly and there stood Mr. Busch. His shiny bald head sat squarely on his long narrow frame. He towered over Phillip in his dark suit, his mustache twitching, and said, "Phillip, why don't you come in and have a seat?" He gestured for Phillip to come inside.

Phillip's legs would not obey him. He stared up at Mr. Busch and thought he'd faint. All his life he'd never even had a timeout during class. Phillip was sure that Mr. Busch didn't even know who he was until this very second. He tried to stand, his legs wiggling like Jell-O on a plate.

Slowly he made his way into the dark, expansive office. Mr. Busch heaved his large self down on to the wooden chair opposite from Phillip.

"So," Mr. Busch said, "tell me about what happened in class."

Phillip had absolutely no idea what to say. He felt as if his mouth was full of sand and grit. The silence continued.

"You are friends with Cedar, are you not?"

How did he know that? Phillip thought. Do principals know everything? Do they run surveillance videos in classrooms? It seems Mr. Busch did know who he was after all.

"Yes, sir, I am," he squeaked.

"And I'm sure you're really worried, with her being in the hospital and everything that's happened."

"Yes, sir, very worried."

Mr. Busch tapped his fingers slowly on his desk. Thump, thump, thump. Phillip gulped, and unsuccessfully tried to restore moisture to his mouth. What was this towering man going to do?

"Did this have anything to do with why Mrs. Doneaway sent you down here?" His eyes, Phillip noticed, were warm and not scary as he gave Phillip his chance at an explanation.

"Ahh, yes, sir, it did. You see, I'm going to visit with Cedar tonight, and she had all these awful tests done on her today, so I'm worried that she'll be in a lot of pain. I know I wasn't paying attention today in class, and sir, it will never happen again."

Mr. Busch nodded and said, "Give Cedar my best tonight, okay?"

Phillip wasn't sure he was done. That couldn't

be all the big and powerful principal would do, could it? Mr. Busch motioned Phillip to the door.

"Thank you, Mr. Busch." And then Mr. Busch actually smiled as Phillip walked out the door. Phillip shook his head in disbelief.

The bell rang for the end of the day, and Phillip rushed into his classroom to grab his backpack and avoid Mrs. Doneaway.

"Hey!" Dan said, packing up his backpack, "I'll see you tomorrow morning."

Phillip nodded, "Do you think many people are coming?"

"I have no idea, man, but I'll be there." Dan said again, as he clapped Phillip on the back, and they ran outside for the bus.

Chapter 11

Phillip sat in his room, thinking of how he would convince his parents to drive him to the hospital and leave him there for the night. The whole plan hinged on Phillip getting to the hospital, breaking Cedar out, and having her in the Worcester Woods by daybreak. Many things had to happen in a certain way or there would be no protest at all. And no saving Cedar.

Phillip also thought about how they would get to the trailhead so late. He couldn't call his parents, they certainly wouldn't approve of taking Cedar from the hospital. Could they find a cab? Or would the cab company turn them in as two minors traveling in the middle of the night? One looking very ill and fresh from the hospital?

No, that wouldn't work. Phillip pushed his hands through his hair, fiddled with his glasses. "Jimmy," he said out loud after a few minutes. "That's it!" Jimmy was Phillip's cousin who lived in

Westerfield. He was barely seventeen years old, a bit of a rebel, had his license, and most importantly, had a car.

He grabbed the phone and retreated back to his room, quickly, before his parents noticed. Phillip dialed his cousin Jimmy's phone number and prayed that he was home, and not out cruising the streets of downtown Westerfield.

Phillip didn't want his aunt to recognize his voice, because then he'd have to explain himself, and she'd probably want to talk to his mom. Phillip concentrated on lowering his voice into a scruffy teenage boy's. "Yeah, hello. Is Jimmy around?"

"Yes, hold on." Aunt Amy's voice was impatient and quick.

"What do you want?" Jimmy called into the phone line.

"Hi, ahh, Jimmy, it's me Phillip, your cousin? Just pretend I'm someone else and walk away from your mom, okay?"

"Sure, buddy. What's going on? You okay?"

"Yeah, well, sorta. My, ahhh, friend, Cedar, is really sick. And I think I know what will save her. Can I ask you a big favor?"

"Shoot."

"I was wondering if you could pick us up at Central Vermont Hospital at midnight tonight, and drop us off at the Worcester trailhead. It would be a huge favor, and… " Phillip pulled out his stashed allowance money from his sock drawer, "and I have 20 bucks I could give you for the ride."

"Wow, Phillip, dude, you surprise me. Sure, man, I'll do that for you, no problem."

"Really? Now this is top secret. And, we could be being chased, so, will you make sure to be there exactly at midnight?"

"With the getaway car, you got it."

Phillip felt like the mastermind of a large crime. If his parents or the hospital busted him he would be in the deepest trouble of his life. A shiver of deep fear ran up through his spine.

Next he had to convince his parents to let him spend the night at the hospital. And the only way he could do that was to play "the girlfriend" card. He knew he'd have to do some powerful acting, and probably provide tears. He'd have to share thoughts and feelings he'd never shared with his parents before. The more he thought about it, the more a pit appeared to scoop out his center. He didn't want to lie to his parents, the thought made him sick to his stomach. He took a few deep breaths, and walked out into the living room.

His parents were sitting around the television, watching the evening news. Phillip thought he'd try the approach his parents had used with him on several occasions.

"Hey guys? Can I talk to you?"

Phillip's mom reached for the clicker and turned off the TV. "Sure honey," she said, her eyes growing wide.

His dad looked slightly annoyed, his feet sprawled out on the couch, the paper stretched across his lap.

"What's up?" his dad said, sitting up.

"Well, as you know, Cedar's in the hospital. And today she had lots of tests—tests with needles and x-rays and who knows what. Last night she didn't want me to leave, and I didn't want to either."

Phillip's mom shot his dad a look.

"I'm really unable to concentrate, to do anything, really." He looked at each of them, sprouting tears in his eyes, "I'm just worried sick." All of this was true. He hadn't lied to them at all. "I just want to go up there and sit in the room with her. To just be there if she wakes up and wants to talk about it at all, whatever. Just to be there."

Phillip's mom came over to his side and rubbed his back. "What do you mean, honey, for visiting hours again? Aren't those over for the night?"

"Yes, but I want to sit with her the whole night. Just this once. Please, it will make her feel so much better."

"We could stay there with you," his mom offered, and she turned to Phillip's dad.

Phillip thought quickly, "I wouldn't want you to be that uncomfortable all night. Those hospital chairs. I know you have to work in the morning."

"Do you think they'll let you in?"

"I could say I'm bringing her some homework, or maybe you could talk to them about it." Phillip looked up, hopeful, his eyes red and watery.

"Oh Phillip," she said, and hugged him sideways. "I remember my first crush. It was very strong. Of course we'll help you out."

Phillip resisted the urge to blurt out, "It's not

a crush! She's just my friend!" because it wouldn't help his cause.

"Do I get a say in all this?" his dad said.

Phillip and his mom looked up from their hug, worried. "Just make sure you get some flowers on the way," he said, and came over and patted Phillip on the head.

Phillip felt a deep pang of guilt near his heart. They were so nice, and he'd be breaking this girl out of the hospital by daybreak.

Chapter 12

C all if there is any problem, Phillip!" his mom yelled from the car. "Make sure it's okay with everyone!"

Phillip rushed away from the car, and sighed. One lie down. Now he had to think about how he'd get by the orange-lipsticked nurse, past 7:00 P.M., past the clearly marked visiting hours, and stay all night. Before when he thought of the idea, it seemed possible; but now as he approached the double doors of the hospital, he wasn't so sure. The cool wind nipped at the beads of sweat on his brow. He pushed the doors open and held his breath. He strode across the gray hospital carpet, taking giant steps and covering ground. Phillip saw the reception desk and looked wildly around. No one was there. He heard a group of nurses laughing down the hallway, but it was mostly quiet. Phillip pushed by the desk and sailed right to the elevator.

Please don't come back to the desk now, please, Phillip thought, waiting for the elevator door to open. Bing! The door opened up and he started walking in.

"Oh, excuse me!" said a doctor in a white coat, pushing by him.

Phillip's heart leapt almost into his mouth. He managed to mumble something as the door closed behind him. He let out a monstrous sigh once on the elevator and had to get ready to make a bee-line straight to Cedar's room. Would someone stop him? Question him? Could he make up a story on the spot? He'd never been a good liar, never needed to be. Now he wished he could be more like the Evil Miranda in his class, cool under pressure, lying like it was no big deal.

Bing! The third floor. The door pushed open and he strode down the hall, head down. He passed a few people, nurses or doctors, custodians' maybe, but he didn't look up, and they didn't stop him.

Phillip got to room 316 and looked in. Cedar was lying there with her eyes closed. She was peaceful, but as pale as the sheets on which she lay. Her skin had a translucent quality, almost shimmering and clear. Her eyes popped open as he slipped in the door.

"Hi Phillip."

"Hi Cedar, you just keep resting for our big mission tonight. I've got a lot of work to do. All you need to do is signal when you see someone coming and I'll ..."

He looked around.

"Roll under the curtain? Or you could hide behind the bathroom door."

"Okay," Phillip said, looking around and trying to appear confident. He sat on the floor beside the bed, out of sight from the window to the corridor.

After a moment of silence, Phillip asked, "How was today?"

"I don't want to talk about it," she said, her voice quivering.

"I'm sorry."

They sat in silence for a while, except for the hum of the machines in the room.

Phillip clicked away on his laptop, lying on the linoleum floor. What if no one showed, what would they do? Catch a ride back to the hospital? Beg forgiveness? Watch Cedar waste away to nothing? Phillip shivered at the thought just as Cedar reached down and whacked him on the head.

"What?"

"Oh hi, Dr. Jones! How are you tonight?"

Chapter 13

Phillip pushed his laptop under a chair and rolled under the bed in one move. Cedar coughed a bit as he hid, thankfully, because he hit the railing with his shin and was trying to stifle calling out in pain.

"How are you feeling, Cedar?"

"A little better now, Dr. Jones."

"Really. That's great! Any idea why?" He came around to check her blood pressure. His foot was barely an inch from Phillip's nose. Phillip tried not to breathe.

"I'm just feeling a bit more positive is all," Cedar said, and the doctor took a small step to the right, reaching for the equipment at Cedar's bedside. His foot came down right on Phillip's extended finger, pressing it into the cold linoleum floor. Phillip sucked in air, suppressing his gasps and wailing. Phillip felt the pain shoot down his hand and into his arm like a shot. The white-hot pain made his stomach reel. Big wet tears filled his eyes. The doctor shifted his weight off Phillip's hand and looked down just as Phillip pulled it under the bed.

Cedar jumped in, "Oh, Dr. Jones, I think it's from all the great care I've been getting here." He looked up at her and smiled.

"Don't worry, Cedar, we'll find out what's bothering you, we will. You just rest and keeping thinking positively, okay?" He winked at her and left.

Phillip moaned from under the bed.

"Are you okay? What happened?"

Phillip rolled out from under the bed, clutching the red tip of his index finger tightly to his chest.

"Yeah, I'm fine," he said through clenched teeth.

"That was close."

He took a couple of deep breaths and looked at his watch. 10:37. Less than an hour and a half before they needed to meet Jimmy in front of the hospital. Phillip shook his hand out and rubbed his finger. No time to worry about it. Then he took out his laptop and opened the file labeled "hospital floor plan."

"Cedar, we need to go over this in detail in case we get separated on the way out."

Phillip packed up his laptop and gathered his things. The clock read 11:37.

"Okay, Cedar, are you ready?" He looked up at her and saw her staring at the plastic tube coming from her wrist. The tube led to a needle stuck into her arm. She shook her head.

"What do I do about this?" she said.

"Why didn't you think of this before!" He wished he could take the words back as soon as he said them.

She stared at him silently, hurt.

"I'm sorry. I just thought we'd worked everything out."

Tears pushed into Cedar's eyes. "I don't know if I can do this. What if I don't make it?"

Phillip slid his hand into hers. "You will make it. Now let's see if we can pull this out."

She nodded, and looked away. Phillip knew it was up to him. He felt the place where the IV needle stuck into Cedar's wrist. The tubing was attached to the needle, and could be replaced. If he only knew how to remove it without hurting her. He could leave the needle in, even though it would be uncomfortable, and just free her from the tubing.

"Just pull!" Cedar said, her eyes scrunched up.

Phillip twisted and pulled out the tube. Cedar drew in a quick breath and the fluid squirted out from the IV all over the bed. Phillip reached for it as it whirled around like a wild snake. He finally grabbed it, pinched the end, knotted it, and attached it to the metal pole where the bag of fluid hung.

"All right, we're in it now Cedar, we have to go!"

"Just hang on." Cedar pushed a paper towel on to the break in her skin where the IV had been. She held it there and gave him a quick nod.

Phillip threw his jacket over Cedar's hospital gown and they headed for the door. Cedar clutched her wrist as Phillip peered down the hallway both ways. His heart hammered in his chest, pounding a steady beat. I can't believe we are really doing this, he thought, I'm going to be arrested. My future is over. They began scurrying down the hallway, like criminals on the loose. Cedar walked just behind Phillip, leaning into his back. As if just being close would make this work, make her stronger. Their fast footfalls clapped on the hard floor, and they heard the intercom call out.

"Code 66 in room 305!"

And the hospital came to life. Doors opened everywhere, voices and footsteps could be heard all around them. Motion, all toward one room with an emergency. Was it them?

"In here!" Phillip called, and they ducked into a room and shut the door behind them. Doctors and nurses walked briskly down the hallway outside. Phillip sighed with relief until Cedar said slowly, "Phillip?"

He turned around and saw an old woman with a shock of white hair, laying in her hospital bed, her hands wrapped around the button that you can press to get immediate assistance in your room. Her thumb was raised as if she were about to press the red button, and her eyes were wide. She had an oxygen mask covering her face, her white hair framed her deeply lined features. Her green eyes were bright, though, alive and could see straight through them it seemed.

"Uh, hi. I'm so sorry to burst into your room

like this. We were just out for a walk in the halls, and…" Cedar stammered.

"And I really don't like people that much, especially people in white coats in hospitals where they stick you with needles, and do other uncomfortable things…" Phillip continued.

"They really just scare him, ma'am, so we thought we'd just duck in here while they all go by. We're really sorry to disturb you."

The woman nodded. She still held tightly to the attention button.

"We'll be gone in just a second, ma'am. Thank you for not getting us in trouble." Phillip said, and they opened the door and headed to the stair well.

"That was a close call!" Cedar cried out.

"Remember, if you see anyone, don't look them in the eye and don't act strange."

"We've got to get outta here. They're going to realize I'm gone soon—if they haven't already. Someone usually comes in at 11:30 to check my blood."

They made it to the stair well door and pushed it open. Clambering down the first set of steps, they heard someone coming up. Phillip kept going, and whispered, "Stay calm," behind him.

But Cedar was gone. A side door clicked closed, and Phillip saw the people coming up from below him. Surely they had heard him by now. He had no choice but to keep going. What had she done? He looked at his watch 11:53. Seven minutes to make it out to Jimmy. What if Cedar couldn't get out? Or she was found and dragged back to her room? Everything would be ruined, everything they had worked for. Most importantly, Cedar would suffer and maybe never make it …

Phillip did the only thing he could do. He looked down and kept going. His mind was about to burst; he felt like he was abandoning her, the most important thing in the world to him. But this was the plan if they got separated. Just keep going and meet up outside. The people coming up the stairs walked right by him, barely noticing this boy, probably caught up in some drama of their own.

He would have Jimmy wait for Cedar. She has to make it out, he thought. We studied the hospital, she can do this. But she also had on a hospital gown, so that if anyone saw her, they'd know she shouldn't be out wandering on the stairs or in the lobby. Phillip shuddered as he reached the bottom floor. He should have brought clothes for her to change into!

Phillip didn't even notice the reception desk as he walked out, deep in thought about Cedar, worried beyond belief.

"Excuse me?" called the orange-lipsticked nurse from behind the desk. "Excuse me? Isn't it a little late to be here, young man?"

He kept walking. He'd never ignored an adult's direct questions and order before. Somehow he was too overcome with what might happen to even bother. Everything might be ruined anyhow, what did it matter?

Chapter 14

Jimmy's black Camaro sat idling in the hospital turnaround. Unbelievable! The kid who was never on time for a class in his life was on time for the getaway. Maybe he knew a serious situation when he heard one.

Phillip opened the door and got in the back seat. "Everything all right dude?"

Phillip pushed his glasses up on his nose. "No. My friend should be out here any minute. We got separated."

"Okay," Jimmy eyed him in the rearview mirror and whistled, "Man, what have you gotten yourself into?"

It was 12:04. Phillip watched in pain as the minutes went by. Jimmy sighed a few times and turned up the music. Phillip kept picturing them finding Cedar, and dragging her back to her room. Calling her parents, giving her medication to make her sleepy and sedated. Taking the life right out of her. Tears sprouted in his eyes and he looked away from Jimmy. Maybe this was a colossal mistake. He could hear his heart hammering in his chest, pounding in his ears.

"Dude, I can't wait here all night."

"Just a couple minutes, Jimmy, please. I'll give you more money."

"How much?"

"Ten more bucks?" That's all Phillip had in his pocket.

Jimmy shrugged.

Just then the automatic double doors burst open, and there was Cedar, brown mane of hair flapping behind her. She was running, like a pale ghost in the dark night. Right behind her was the orange-lipsticked nurse, her bun coming undone, huffing after her. Phillip threw open the back door and Cedar dove in.

"GO! GO! GO!" Phillip yelled, pulling Cedar's door closed. She had flung herself across the back seat, and now lay there, eyes closed, breath rapidly rising and falling.

"Oh Jesus," Jimmy said as they sped away from the nurse, who stood waving and yelling.

"Cedar, Cedar are you okay? I didn't know what to do back there. I wasn't sure if I should leave you or go back. I didn't want to blow your cover and I didn't know where you'd gone."

"Dude, slow down, she's okay. Just give her a minute. I can't believe you guys." Jimmy shook his head. In all of his class-skipping days, he'd never had a getaway that close before.

Cedar's breathing slowed. Her skin was even paler then before, and cold sweat dripped from her forehead. "I'm okay," she said, sitting up slightly. "I hid in a storage closet until those people went by. Once I was down in the lobby that lady started asking me questions and I just made a break for it."

"You guys, the cops will be after you now. You better hope that you can do whatever it is you need to do before they find you."

Phillip gulped. This was the voice of an expert. Of course the nurse would call the cops. Once they found Cedar's room empty, they'd have two runaway minors on the loose. And a witness to them actually leaving. Phillip's gut wrenched. What if the cops got to them first? Would they go to jail? Would they send them off to juvenile boot camp school forever? Phillip tried to push these thoughts from his head as he looked back at Cedar.

She hunched there, her body worn, but her eyes were strong and as steady, like an ancient forest. She knew what they had to do. Of course. She was braver then he'd ever be.

Jimmy turned his lights off as they drove down Bear Swamp Road. He didn't want Phillip's or Cedar's family to see his car if they were awake and had already been called by the hospital. Phillip knew it wouldn't be long before they would figure out where they went. He just hoped that they could stage the protest for a little while before they hauled him off.

It was now after 1 A.M. They had only six hours until Cedar's life, their future and the future of the Worcester Woods would be determined forever.

Chapter 15

Jimmy opened the door to a symphony of night sounds. He leaned over and said, "Are you sure you guys will be all right?" He motioned into the deep woods. "Cuz it's really dark out there."

"We'll be fine, Jimmy, thanks."

"Okay. Good luck, dude." Jimmy reached out and shook Phillip's hand. Phillip saw the surprise in Jimmy's eyes, the new respect he had for him.

The door pulled shut, and the Camaro's tires crunched slowly down the road. Phillip watched the taillights fade until they were down the hill and out of sight. Now they were in total darkness. Cedar's eyes were barely open, her presence seemed tiny and fragile. A sliver moon gave off the thinnest of light to see by.

They walked silently down the trail, Phillip feeling disconnected from his body. Once they were engulfed in the trees, and the moonlight did not reach them, Phillip stopped and bent over his backpack. He pulled out a flashlight.

"No, Phillip." Cedar's hand went to his. "We need our eyes to get used to the dark, for them to get adjusted, then we'll be fine. This way we'll be able to see more."

"Are you crazy? Then anything can sneak up on us! A bear, a coyote."

"Shhhh! Phillip, its okay. Nothing will hurt us out here, I promise. All the animals are well aware of our presence. They mean no harm and want to be left alone." He nodded his okay.

Phillip walked ahead, crunching leaves under his feet. Noises ahead on the trail stopped as they neared. The chorus of crickets silenced as they walked by. Phillip's heart hammered against his chest. He tried not to turn around to check if anything was following them. The sliver of moon appeared over the trees. The temperature cooled, and Phillip realized the chattering he heard was coming from Cedar.

"Take my jacket. Why didn't you tell me you were cold?" He slid his fleece around her shoulders and felt her spine through her thin hospital gown.

He looked at Cedar, who was barely awake. Her long brown hair, matted and knotted, flew behind her. She walked in her hospital gown and now Phillip's thick fleece. Her long, deer-like legs were pale and smooth in the moonlight. It was amazing that this little person had so much strength, so much will. He flushed as he thought about her frail, beautiful body.

Before them rose Stella, the great Cedar, almost glowing in the moonlight. Cedar walked right over to her, to the curved roots that cradled her long ago, and lay down. Phillip followed, putting down his pack and taking out a sleeping bag and blankets he had packed. Cedar curled up in the blankets and leaned back. Her eyes closed immediately.

Phillip sat partially covered with the blanket. He didn't want to invade her space, but he was not comfortable at all. His mind raced with the possibilities of all the things that could be happening at this very moment. Police cars looking for them. Calls being made to their houses, their parents alarmed and worried. Phillip pushed his glasses up his nose, looking around. The trees stood silent, their orange ribbons bobbing gently in the night breeze. A stillness settled around them, and he looked over at Cedar.

She lay curled on one side, her back cradled in the reaching, curving roots of Stella, the mighty Cedar. Her face looked almost translucent, glowing, and utterly peaceful. Her lips were curled up in a small smile, and she looked more at home and comfortable than Phillip had ever seen her. And more beautiful.

It was crazy, what they were doing, and he knew it. But deep down in his soul he knew it was the right thing to do. He couldn't explain why. It was like how you know when someone is looking at you, even before you see him or her. The plan *had* to work. He hadn't thought about what would happen if it didn't. If Cedar became gravely ill, or worse— he couldn't even begin to imagine.

He stared at her for a long time, before she sighed lightly and moved a bit. He jumped out of embarrassment and fright and nearly screamed. It took him several moments to recover his normal breathing. Even then, he never fully recovered. The woods were Cedar's home, not his. Sure, he learned to like it, but he didn't feel comfortable, or safe, especially on this night when he knew many people would be looking for them soon.

Phillip looked around. The crescent moon provided just enough filtered, milky light to see the varying shapes of the reaching, towering trees around them. From the ground the branches hung over them like a maze, and stars peeked through the holes, twinkling. The trees, Phillip had learned, were sugar maples, cedars, white pines, beech and birch, and were all valuable for their wood.

But their value was so much more than that.

As he watched her sleep, he knew that these trees were worth everything he and Cedar had done. They'd given oxygen, homes to animals, life to the forest, and to Cedar. Their value was so much greater than a mere dollar amount. Phillip had learned that a Cedar tree, in Latin, means "tree of life." This was certainly true for Cedar. Not just that, but Cedars had been used for centuries for the medicinal properties of their sap, bark and twigs. This tree, all trees really, held magic, medicine, and life. How could he explain this? How would anyone ever understand?

Would anyone come?

He had sent emails to every TV station for miles around, to every student at Chester school, even to local politicians whom he found on the Internet. What if they all laughed it off as some stupid kids acting out a fantasy they created? What then?

Phillip's stomach rumbled loudly. He hadn't been able to eat anything at dinner, and now he felt intermittently hungry and nauseous. He dug around as quietly as he could in his pack, searching for some forgotten snack, a crushed-up energy bar, crackers, something.

And that's when he heard it.

Chapter 16

Asqueal and a yip pierced the night, shooting fear like an electric shock throughout Phillip's body. From deep in the woods came more yips, squeals, and then eventually, a howl.

They weren't alone.

While Cedar snoozed on, serenely tucked into her birth tree, Phillip thought his heart would burst. He popped up, squinting into the cool night. Of course he could see nothing. Even with his headlamp, the beam didn't go far very into the night. Only a few feet of forest floor were illuminated.

Coyotes. Would they come for him? For Cedar? He shivered, gulped.

But then he turned and looked back at Cedar. She was almost glowing under the soft moonlight, tucked in around her tree. So comfortable. So trusting.

She had said that the animals knew when humans are present—all the time. They are more scared of us then we are of them. Right now, he wasn't so sure about that. He walked back over and sat right next to Cedar. As he heard more yips and howls he sunk in next to her, trying to slow his breathing. They were together, in these woods to-night. He never thought he could do anything like he did that day. No one could take this away, no matter what.

At any moment, they could be coming for them. Police, doctors, their parents, or teachers. As the howls in the distance called on, Phillip just tried to listen. They were electric, alive, fierce. Just as he was on this night. Every cell of him felt awake, open, waiting.

He reached over and took Cedar's hand. He wouldn't sleep. He wanted to be ready for what happened next. The fall night danced around him—cool, crisp air, owls calling, coyotes in the distance. And he was a part of it.

Sometime in between the worlds of day and night—the gray time when shapes move from behind shadows, Phillip fell asleep.

That is, until leaves crunched and a twig snapped. Someone was coming. And both Cedar and Phillip slept sweetly under Stella, barely visible in the grey and dawning light.

Chapter 17

Phillip's eyes popped open, his brain trying to clear the fog of sleep and see in the veiled dawn light. Feet on leaves, moving closer.

Phillip jumped to his feet. He had an urge to run and hide, but as he looked at Cedar, still fast asleep, he knew he could not leave her. He needed to face what was coming.

Then he wanted to fight. For some reason, each cell in his being wanted to run up and tackle whoever was coming closer. Just knock him or her right over, and show who was boss.

He shook his head. That didn't make any sense. So he crouched, and waited as the light leaked brighter by the second.

A shrugging silhouette appeared, looking not much larger than Phillip. And as he approached, a digital light glowed, showing some of his face.

Phillip relaxed back into the tree. Not an enemy. Not at all.

"Dude. That is one beautiful tree," he whispered as he approached, awestruck.

His classmate Dan Bloom had showed up. And he was taking streaming video.

❀

While Cedar slept, Dan interviewed Phillip about the forest, about Cedar, The Order, and the development. Phillip didn't hold anything back. In the morning light, he told Dan everything that had happened, about their harrowing escape, and about how Cedar looked so much healthier now that she was home with her tree—and that they had to save this very forest to keep her alive.

Dan sat down afterward and Cedar slowly came to. She rubbed her eyes, and even though she had been so sick, her light was back, and the blistering intensity of her eyes shined on Dan and Phillip seated under Stella.

"How are you feeling?" Phillip asked, eyebrows pinched together in concern.

"So much better here. Thank you, Phillip," she looked toward Dan, "and welcome to my home,

Dan, so glad you could make it. You may very well be the only other member of our protest."

"Oh, I don't think so," Dan said, smirking.

"What do you mean?"

He pointed to the little red light recording Cedar's awakening, her giant eyes shining.

"The world knows you now. Or they soon will."

Chapter 18

Dan clicked on his laptop in the morning light. He was busy writing a blog post all about the morning: biking to the trailhead, finding Cedar and Phillip in the dawn, learning about the Order, about Cedar's connection and how it was linked to the development. In a few minutes, it was live, on-line, with embedded video.

"What happens now?" Phillip asked.

"We wait. We see what happens," said Dan, leaning back into Stella.

By now it was 6:00 A.M., and Dan had brought a thermos of hot chocolate and some energy bars. They ate thankfully.

"It won't be long now, Cedar. Our parents must know…"

"Cedar?"

"Dude, where'd she go?"

"Hey there, up here!"

Cedar had climbed up Stella like she was a set of stairs. She made her way causally out to one of the thickest limbs, about 20 feet up in the air.

"What are you doing! Be careful—remember all that pain, you've been so sick!" Phillip's worry rushed out of his mouth like a river.

"I feel so good. Nothing can harm me here. Plus, I do this all the time."

Dan and Phillip stood under the tree, necks angled back, staring at the marvel moving among the branches.

"See this little pocket of branches? This is my reading spot. I've been coming here for ages. I bring a book, sometimes a blanket and read up here for hours. It is so peaceful, just the birds, the breeze."

"Cedar! Phillip!" came from a distance away. The tone echoed off the rocks, the trees.

Serious adult voices shattered Cedar's explanation. Her face changed completely and she made her way quickly down, like a monkey moving with ease through a tree.

Phillip and Cedar looked at each other. It was time to face whoever was coming.

Chapter 19

They stood in front of Stella, together. Dan Bloom stood a bit back, cell phone in hand. He was not going to miss any of this.

"Thank God!" Cedar's mom called as they ran toward the three kids. Sara Montgomery's face was one of sheer panic. Hollowed eyes, disheveled hair, creases between her eyebrows.

"I thought, I thought…" she hugged Cedar tightly.

Phillip's parents emerged as part of the group and looked at Phillip in a way he had never seen.

"We trusted you. How could you do this? She is so sick!" yelled his dad. His mom looked on, shaking her head.

"Stop, everyone. It is not Phillip's fault. He was trying to help me."

"Help you?" said Sara Montgomery, "how can breaking you out of the hospital help you! What were you thinking!"

Phillip's dad said, "Get your stuff. We are leaving. You've done enough damage here."

Cedar took her mom's hands. Tipped up her chin.

"Mom, look at me. Look at my face."

Cedar's mom turned to look at her daughter.

"See me. See my eyes. You know it is true."

Tears sprouted in Sara Montgomery's eyes as she looked deep into the fiery, deer-like eyes of her wild tree daughter. She knew in that moment the way you know things. The way you feel love like a blanket.

"Kevin. Look at Cedar. She is bright. She is well."

"But how can that be?" Cedar's dad marveled.

"Because she is home. Because her fate is connected to this tree." At this, Cedar's parents paused, eyes locked on Cedar.

Phillip's dad interrupted the silence. "I have no idea what you all are talking about, but I have to get to work, and this boy here is grounded for life, so if you don't mind, he's coming with me."

"Dad, I can't leave. We've made it this far. Cedar's mom is right."

"Um, excuse me," Dan Bloom called.

"Young man, you are coming with me." Phillip's dad reached and caught Phillip's arm.

"Let go! I was only trying to help!"

"You'd better turn around, folks," Dan said, camera raised and recording.

Behind the group, dozens of people were coming forward, many holding signs, calling into the forest.

"Save the Worcester Woods! Save Cedar!"

"Save the Worcester Woods! Save Cedar!"

They kept coming. Piles of kids holding hand-lettered signs. Parents holding their kids' hands. It seemed that Chester School had emptied and appeared right on the trail, right in the woods before them.

The adults were speechless, and Cedar broke into a wide smile. The morning light bathed the dozens of families that emerged around Stella. Cedar and Phillip stepped around the stunned adults and started greeting classmates, teachers, parents, friends, and many people they didn't know.

Cedar looked around, light as air, in disbelief. Phillip ran his hands through his hair, whispered, "Unbelievable."

They didn't even notice the TV news cameras.

Chapter 20

The group kept chanting, and then stopped to listen to Phillip and Cedar.

"I cannot believe you all came," Phillip called out, choking on the words, "We really appreciate you."

As he spoke, Mr. Bausch showed up behind the group, followed by several adults in nice clothes.

"… You must have some belief in us, in Cedar, and in the magic of these woods to get up so early and come out here," Phillip called.

Cedar looked up and out on the crowd. She said, "We know little about how our environment is tied to us all. Maybe not as strongly as I am to this place, but each one of us is intricately tied to our water, our land, our home. By helping protect this forest, you protect not only my home, but yours. Our forests clean our air, they take our anxiety away, they teach us about nature and resilience, about renewal and strength. All of which I have needed in recent days, and we will all need often in our lives."

The group encircled Stella, listening, building in numbers. More people trickled in, gathering around the towering tree.

"This is only the beginning. We will need to fight to make sure this forest is not cut down, for me but also for you, and we all need to work together to protect forests and habitats everywhere."

As she spoke Cedar was electric. The crowd listened raptly as her fearless eyes stared out at them. Her strength seemed to be shooting out, reaching like branches into their eyes and hearts and minds.

Chapter 21

As she spoke, Dan pulled on Phillip's arm.

"Dude, you'd better look at this."

Dan had started a Save the Worcester Woods Facebook page. It had over 1,000 members, and it had only been on-line one hour.

"Look at the comments."

"Hello, this is Channel Nine News, we've just heard of your protest and would like to interview you...."

"Hi, this is your local representative. I'd like to speak to you about your campaign to save this forest."

"Hello, this is NPR. We read your blog post on Huffington Post Youth and would like to interview you for our radio program. . . ."

"Greetings, my name is Amy from the Forest Stewardship Council. We want to support your work to preserve this forest. . . ."

And the list went on and on.

Phillip and Dan read, jaws dropping.

Meanwhile, as Cedar closed her comments, the crowd erupted in applause.

Mr. Bausch approached quickly with two other adults.

"Phillip, Cedar, I am so glad to see that you are all right! You gave us quite a scare."

Phillip smiled his small smile. Mr. Bausch continued, "I want to introduce you to two of your town select board representatives. They granted the approval of this development and are interested in hearing more about your side of things."

With that he winked.

Phillip knew Mr. Bausch was a good guy.

The town representative spoke first, combed dark hair bobbing, "While we appreciate your efforts here, this development is perfectly legal, and, unfortunately, the forest clearing will begin today." He looked in physical pain to be standing in the woods with all of these people.

Cedar's eyes were burning holes in the representative, and Phillip stammered, put off by the condescending tone of the man and struggled for words. Dan looked up and smiled.

"While we appreciate *you* coming out here, you are going to have to answer to all of these people who want to save this forest," he waved his hand to the cheering crowd, "and to all of these people, too." He held up his computer, showed the town selectman the page and the comments. Then someone else tapped the representative on the shoulder, and a video camera was shoved in his face.

A news reporter had pushed her way into the scene, her videographer right beside her. "Are you a town representative who voted on having this development? What do you plan to do to save this girl and preserve this forest? Will you ignore the will of the people here today?"

Visibly stunned, the representative said "No comment!" and started walking briskly away. Dan smiled. The news media was here, and they weren't going away. While the fight ahead to save the forest might be long, today, they were winning.

Cedar, Phillip, and Dan sighed in relief, and laughed a little. They hugged their parents, who were now, at last, accepting what was happening.

They looked up at the mighty Stella, and all of her tree family, bathed in late morning light, surrounded by hope and beauty and change.

Epilogue

THAT WAS THE DAY that changed everything. The news media far and wide covered the story of two kids who started a protest to save their forest, and the girl who was found as a baby in it. Donations came pouring in from all over the world into a Save the Worcester Woods fund set up by Cedar's parents. The Town Council put the development on hold, and Cedar's health improved. At the hearing later that month, Cedar's parents had raised enough money both locally and on-line that they simply bought the land, and turned it into a park for all the residents of Middlesex, Worcester, and beyond.

Cedar's health blossomed. She seemed to grow like the trees that were newly protected. The fire in her eyes was back, her long limbs stretching and growing. Phillip emerged as a school leader, the perception of him after the protest changed forever. He stood a little taller. He wasn't afraid to speak up to anyone, any more.

Cedar, Phillip and Dan did start that environmental club at school. Dan started a blog about their work, and a YouTube channel featuring their projects. Soon, they were organizing other campaigns to save local habitats and to demand that companies respect the environment. They had thousands of fans, and they continued to raise money for their work with the fund set up by Cedar's parents.

Dan was welcomed into the Order of the Trees, held each week in the newly formed Worcester Woodland Community Park. They had to limit the membership to 20 local kids, and are considering opening another chapter.

Perhaps, dear reader, you could start your very own chapter of the Order of the Trees. Who knows what kind of magic you will find there?

Reader Guide

1. Due to Cedar's belief that the trees are her forest family, she has personified them by naming them. Do you believe plant species, such as trees, have their own personalities and deserve names?

2. Why is Mrs. Doneaway so harsh when it comes to reprimanding Cedar and Phillip? Does it have something to do with who she favors and who she doesn't? Or is it because Cedar and Phillip are different from the other kids and she is childish when it comes to judging those she doesn't know a lot about?

3. Dan used social media and technology to inform people about the demolishment of the Worcester Woods. Was that a good move on his part? If he hadn't used the Internet to help, would the movement still have gotten the attention it did?

4. Were Cedar's and Phillip's parents' reactions acceptable when they made it to the Worcester Woods?

5. Even if Cedar and the link between her living and dying was not connected to Stella and the rest of the trees, do you think Phillip still would have done so much to try and save the forest?

6. Do you agree with Cedar when she says the forest is an escape? Do you spend a lot of time in the forest as well?

7. Because some trees have longer life-spans than the average human, does that mean Cedar will have a prolonged

life? Or is it possible that she will live a normal life and Stella will only serve as her life support for as long as Cedar needs it? And when Cedar becomes old and it is time for her to pass, will Stella pass away with her?

8. Do you know of any environmental groups in your area? Are you or someone you know a part of one?

9. How does Cedar react to the malicious things Miranda and Sam say and do? How does Phillip react? Why do you think Miranda and Sam are so mean to them?

10. Would you have helped saved the Worcester Woods with Cedar and Phillip?

11. Is it possible for Cedar to be a child of the forest? She has an unexplainable connection with the Worcester Woods. Could it possibly be something otherworldly, something magical? Or just a strong love for nature and the trees?

12. The story goes that Cedar was found at the base of a tree, whom we now know as Stella. Is it possible that the trees sent Cedar in order to save them? And if so, did they work some sort of spell on Phillip to help Cedar?

13. At the beginning of the novel, Phillip is a little hesitant to accept the invitation for joining The Order of the Trees. How do his views of the forest change? Why?

14. Compare and contrast Phillip at the beginning and end of the novel. How and why has he changed?

15. Besides keeping Cedar and The Order safe, why was it important for Phillip to save the Worcester Woods? Why is it important to save any kind of forest?

16. If you had the chance to save a forest, would you?

17. Do you think Phillip gained the confidence he had to save his friend and the forest by becoming friends with Cedar? Or did he have it within him all along?

18. Was it right for Phillip to lie and break the law so he could save his friend and The Order?

CPSIA information can be obtained at www.ICGtesting.com
Printed in the USA
LVOW11s2053190415

435235LV00006B/8/P

9 780990 973317